CAPTAIN
Sparklebeard

Timothy Knapman & Sam Lloyd

EGMONT

There was once a girl called **Peg**.
She lived by the sea with her wicked
Step-Great-Grand Auntie.

"Sweep the floor!"
the old woman
commanded.

"Mend my
clothes!

Polish
my jewels
till they
sparkle!"

Peg's room

Peg worked hard all day long,
but at night she read **pirate stories**,
and dreamed of **escape** and **adventure**.

Then one day, when Peg took
her wicked Step-Great-Grand Auntie's
cat for a walk, she saw . . .

the pirates had come to town!

"We have a treasure map!" roared Captain Hairy-Ears.

"Anybody who dreams of escape and adventure can join our crew!"

But when Peg asked to join their crew,
ever so nicely, Captain Hairy-Ears said,

"No. Pirates don't ask nicely.

Pirates aren't small.

And all pirates have beards!"

"But I've
read lots of
pirate stories!"
said Peg.

"Whoever heard
of a pirate who can read?"
said Captain Hairy-Ears.
And he laughed a smelly pirate
laugh, "Hurr-hurr-hurr!"

No one was going to ruin Peg's chance of escape
and adventure, so that night, she worked.

She made a pirate outfit from curtains . . .

. . . and a big bushy beard out of the floor brush.
It itched a bit, but she REALLY wanted to show those pirates.

Then she saw the jewels
that she'd polished, **sparkling**.

And she had an **idea**.

The next morning, the pirates saw a brand new pirate in a boat made of books!

"Who on sea are you?" asked Captain Hairy-Ears.

"I am Captain Sparklebeard!"
said Peg. "The greatest pirate there
ever was! And whatever it takes,
I will find that treasure before you do!"

"Whoever heard of a boat made of **books**?" roared Captain Hairy-Ears. "One splosh of water and you'll **sink**!"

"Don't you know books are made from **trees**, just like pirate ships?" said Peg.

"If you tie enough together you can sail the Seven Seas forever and a day."

The pirates laughed their
smelly pirate laugh,
"Hurr-hurr-hurr"
and sailed off.

BIG BOOK OF
SEA PERILS

"Grrr," said Peg
and she opened her
Big Book of Sea Perils.

The book said that there was a wild
and whirling **whirlpool**
on the way to the island.

Shiver me timbers,
whirlpool
ahead!

Buckle up,
me hearties.

So Peg put on her seatbelt and she didn't get
whooshed and slooshed around.

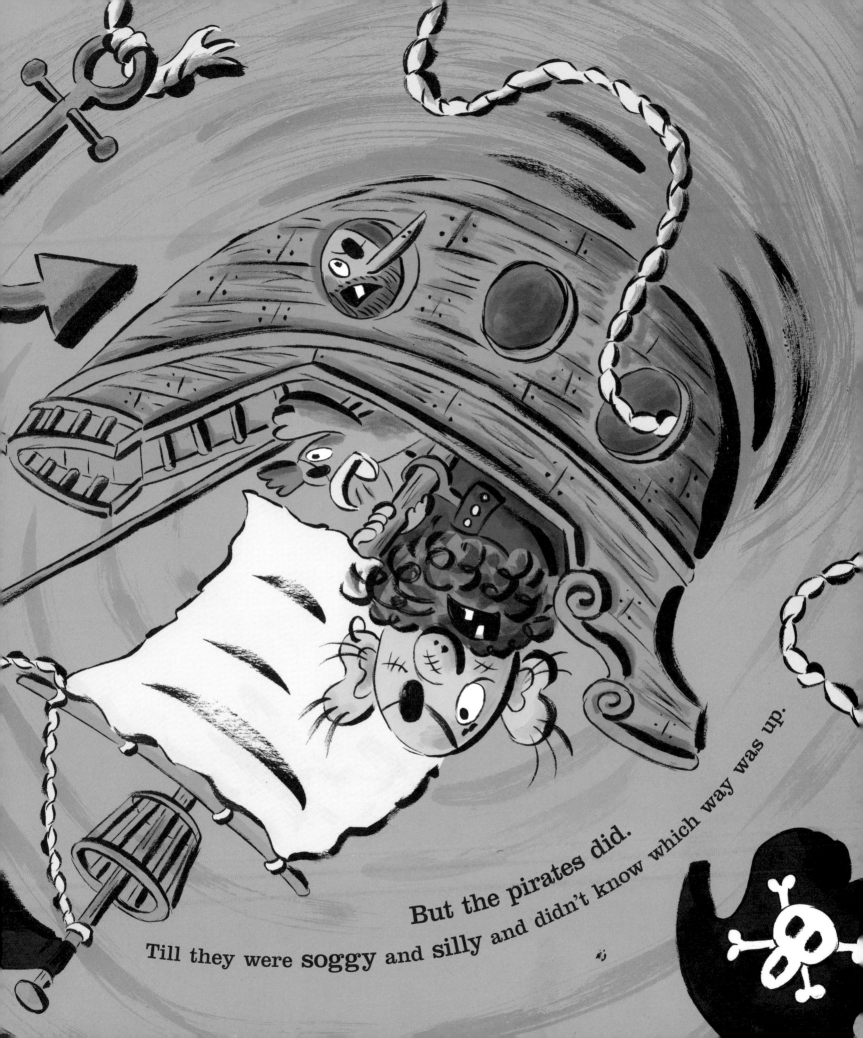

But the pirates did.

Till they were **soggy** and **silly** and didn't know which way was up.

The book said that there was a slimy and snappy
sea serpent ready to spring out
and swallow you.

OO - ARR! There be a sea serpent Scallywag ahead.

Dazzle dem eyes, ye landlubber.

So Peg dazzled it with the light from her **sparkling** beard
and she didn't get chased rotten and chomped ragged.

But the pirates did.

Till they were scared **silly**
and shaking like jellyfish.

The book also said that there was . . .

N
W · **E**
S

yo-ho-ho!
Full steam
ahead!

an underwater
volcano,

razor-sharp rocks

and beastly bottom
barnacles.

So Peg knew exactly how to avoid
them and she didn't arrive at the island
looking like a nervous wreck.

Treasure
Island

But the pirates did.

"Grrr," they said.

And "Ouch, my bottom!"

And "What are you doing here?"

marks the spot

X

X

Raffle Snake Rocks

"I'm going to find that treasure before you," said Peg.

"But we still have the **map**!" said Captain Hairy-Ears, waving it weakly in Peg's face.

The pirates were too wobbly to laugh their smelly pirate laugh, so they just limped off to find the treasure.

They searched all over the island . . .

Rattlesnake Rocks

Crocodile Canyon

from bitey jungle

to blizzardy mountains.

Bone Beach

Piranha Pool

"We give up," they said at long last. **"Where is it?"**

"It's right here," said Peg. "You showed me your map, but you can't read so you didn't know that it was upside down."

Then she lifted up her beard and said,

"Oh, and I'm a girl by the way!"

"We don't care!" cried Captain Hairy-Ears, bursting into tears. "You're the **greatest** pirate there **ever was**. Please can you teach us how to read and let us join your crew?"

"Of course!" said Peg.
"Because you asked so **nicely**."

Sailed the Seven Seas forever and a day.

Boat O' Books

BIG BOOK OF SEA PERILS

She was small and she read books,
and she was the greatest pirate there ever was.